Icy Magic
Oceana the Ocean Fairy

BY

AANYA GARG

Pharos Books

**Next book
in Icy Magic series**
Anna the Anglerfish Fairy

©Publisher

Publisher: Pharos Books (P) Ltd.
Plot No.-55, Main Mother Dairy Road
Pandav Nagar, East Delhi-110092
Phone: 011-40395855, +14049995474
WhatsApp: +91 8368220032
E-mail: sales@pharosbooks.in
Website: www.pharosbooks.in
First Edition: 2022

Printed By: Sushma Book Binding House, Okhla
Industrial Area, Phase II, New Delhi-110020

Icy Magic: Oceana the Ocean Fairy
Aanya Garg

Books in Icy Magic Series

Ocean fairies

Oceana the Ocean fairy

Anna the Anglerfish fairy

Sophia the Stonefish fairy

Olivia the Octopus fairy

Catlyn the Clownfish fairy

Rosella the Rockfish fairy

Molly the Manatee fairy

Dedicated to

My Nani and Nana
(Mrs. Seema Agarwal & Dr. R.C. Agarwal)

For recognizing the value of my stories and motivating me to publish them. Your vision came true!

CONTENTS

CHAPTER 1

Alice and Christy were on their third day in a two-week summer camp organized by Coral Adventures. The campsite was at Coral Beach in their town Sparkle City, which was just a few blocks away from their home at Snow Towers, Cavanaugh Road.

They were playing frisbee at the beach with their new friends at the camp.

As their frisbee flew near the sea water, Christy exclaimed, "Oh Alice, this looks awful. I don't remember seeing litter the last time we were here."

Alice looked farther down the beach at even more litter floating on the sea and scattering on the sand. "We have to do something about it!" Christy said determinedly.

"I wonder from where all this litter is coming from?" said Alice, scratching her head. They were so absorbed in discussing the ocean pollution that they completely forgot about their frisbee and friends.

Then they saw a small plastic bag glowing on the sand. They went to take a closer look. Suddenly, a fairy came fluttering out from under the plastic bag.

CHAPTER 2

"Oceana!" Alice and Christy whispered to the tiny fairy, "We have been waiting for you."

They quickly understood that the time has

come to find Oceana's magical shell, stolen by

Fireblast. Surely the unusual litter at the beach

was related to Fireblast's misuse of the shell.

Fireblast, a squawker who wanted to rule

Icy Palace, always looked for ways to create

trouble for the fairies by stealing their magical

objects. Squawkers are non-fairy kids born to

fairy parents. They can look like humans, but

unlike humans, they are born with some strange

evil powers and looks. Squawkers can rise to the rank of fairies if they successfully graduate from Fairy Training School and pass the Magic Wand Granting Ceremony. However, Fireblast, who did not believe in hard work did not complete the fairy training. He grew up as a troublemaker and was therefore sent to a far-away land to live.

Nobody in Icy Palace knew where he went. True to his name, Fireblast looked like a scary monster with fiery eyes and spiky red hair. His

teeth were uneven with a flame-shaped pattern.

He held a wand in his one hand. Whenever he

lost his mind, his hair would start to glow with

fire and his eyes would turn pure red.

CHAPTER 3

Oceana said urgently, "Girls, are you ready to undertake your first magical adventure?"

"Yes!" Alice and Christy nodded at once. Oceana swung her wand in the air and a calm white cloud hovered above them, showering golden dust on them. They shrank to fairy size and wings began to sprout from their backs.

They began to fly. With another flick of Oceana's wand, they reached the Icy Palace.

There they met Queen Alexa and King Charles. "Hi!" greeted the girls to the king and queen. "Welcome to the Icy Palace," replied the queen in a calm voice. "I am glad we can rely on your help".

Just last night, Oceana received an alert on her wrist band. It was flashing red, which meant Fireblast was misusing the power of her shell. Let's rush over to the Magic Pond to find the shell's location."

CHAPTER 4

On reaching the Magic Pond, Queen Alexa said the spell to show the girls what had happened. The Magic Pond showed Fireblast sailing in the Pacific Ocean, holding Oceana's ruby shell. He was up to mischief, using Oceana's shell to add more and more trash into the ocean. The power of the shell depends on its wielder.

Since it was in the hands of someone with

bad intentions, its power resulted in evil.

Instead of preventing pollution in the ocean, it

created even more pollution. Queen Alexa said,

"Oceana's ruby shell helps to control the ocean

pollution. But now, all that pollution Fireblast

is adding in the ocean will cause the animals to

choke and suffocate. We need to find the ruby

shell quickly."

Then, with a flick of Oceana's wand, they

were sailing in a boat on the Pacific Ocean.

They saw Fireblast sailing in another boat, intent on creating pollution. When he spotted Oceana and the girls, he pointed his wand and shot a hot gust of wind at them. Oceana shouted, "Now!" Instantly, the girls put their hands on her shoulders.

Oceana instantly felt powerful and used her frost-shield power to create a snowy whirlwind spinning around to protect them from the heat winds.

CHAPTER 5

Shielded, they quickly made a plan to get the ruby shell. They would find another shell and paint it golden to make it look magical. Then, they would exchange the ruby shell for the golden shell. They knew Fireblast was always greedy to have new magical objects for the pleasure of creating mischief.

Oceana said a spell and a shell and golden paint appeared. Christy painted the shell. The girls moved the boat towards Fireblast. Christy held out her hand and said to Fireblast, "Would you like to exchange your ruby shell for this magical golden shell? Fireblast nodded because the golden shell indeed looked magical. He was really tempted. The ruby shell was now of less appeal to him because he had already used it. Then, Christy took the ruby shell and Fireblast took the golden shell.

Christy, Alice and Oceana sailed back towards the seashore away from Fireblast. When Fireblast tried to work the magic of the golden shell it didn't work. He realized that he had been tricked. He shouted furiously back to the girls, "Next time you won't be able to get the other shells back from me!"

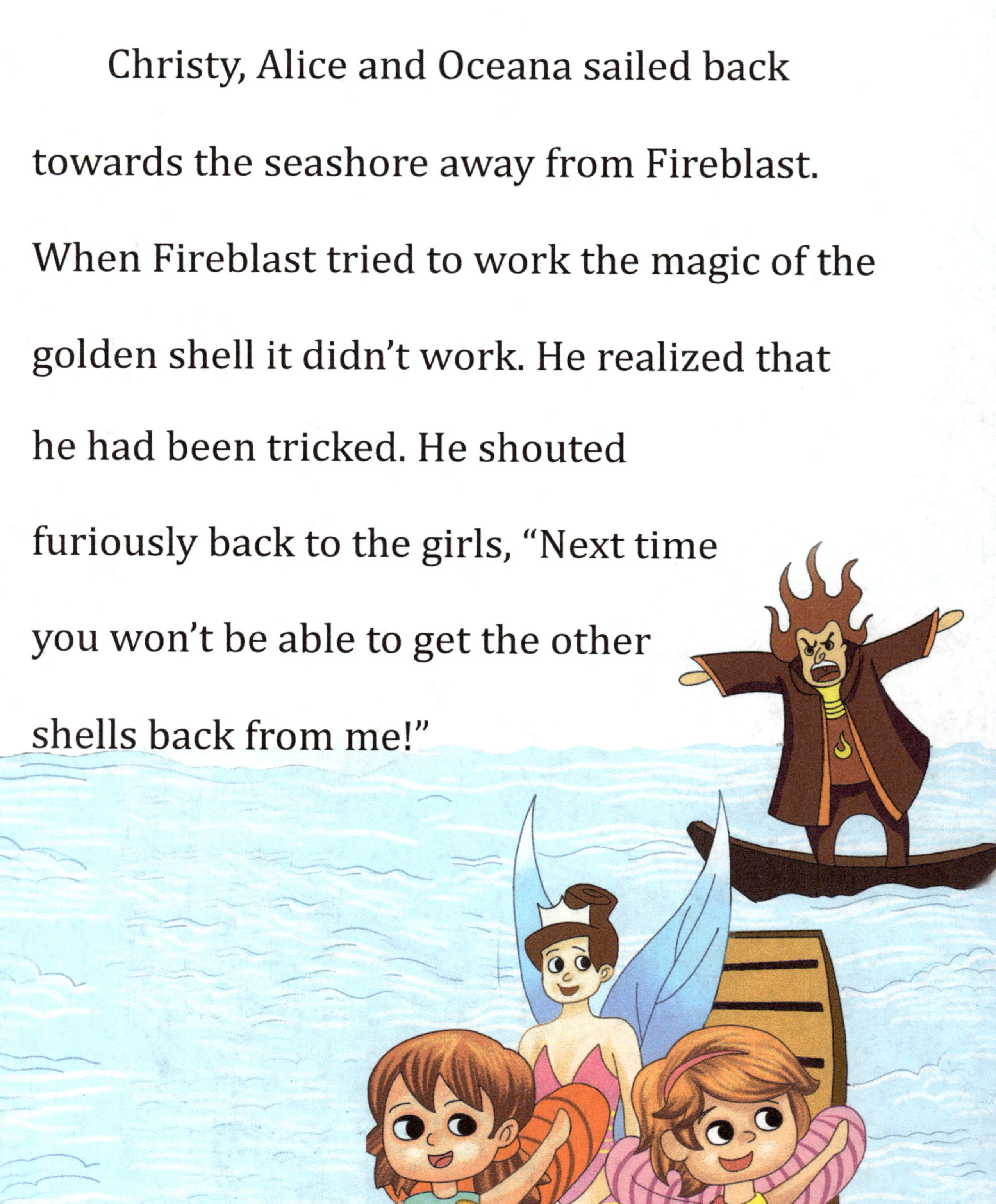

CHAPTER
6

Then Oceana waved her wand in the shape

of ocean waves and they were sent to the Icy

Palace to meet the King and Queen.

Oceana returned her ruby shell to the Queen for safekeeping. Queen Alexa was very happy. I am grateful for your help," Oceana said to the girls. "As soon as the queen finds out about the other shells, we shall send a fairy to summon you to the Icy Palace. But for now, we would have to say goodbye." Alice and Christy hugged Oceana. With a flick of Oceana's wand, they were sent back to the human world. They found themselves standing on the beach with their frisbee beside them. It seemed to them as if

nothing had changed in the human world while they were away on their magical adventure.

Nobody seemed to notice that Alice and Christy were gone on a fairy adventure.

One shell is found but the other six shells are still missing. Things are only going to get more difficult and trickier!

Beep...Beep...Anna the Anglerfish Fairy receives an alert on her wrist band: the topaz shell is being misused. Do you think Alice and Christy

will be able to help Anna get back her topaz

shell? What ocean trouble lies ahead? What will

be their next shell rescue plan? Will they be

successful? Read on in the next book: Anna the

Anglerfish Fairy.

FUN FACTS

1. **Pacific Ocean is home to 75% of earth's volcanoes!** Most of the volcanoes on earth are located underwater, along the aptly named "Ring of Fire" in the Pacific Ocean. Running in the shape of horseshoe, much around the rim of Pacific Ocean, "Ring of Fire" stretches up to 25,000 miles long and contains 75% of the world's active volcanoes. 90% of Earth's earthquakes also occur along this path.

2. **The Pacific Ocean is home to more than 25,000 Islands!** Most of the world's islands – including Hawaii are located in Pacific Ocean.

3. **The Great Pacific Garbage Patch!** Pacific Ocean, which contains the Great Pacific Garbage Patch, is one of the most polluted oceans in the world. The main culprit for the pollution is microplastics- small fragments of plastic which float in the water. This island-sized patch contains everything from water bottle to tires, desk chairs & cell phones. It holds around 2 trillion plastic pieces & contain about 1/3rd of all the plastic pollution in the world's oceans.

4. **Pacific Ocean is home to the Great Barrier Reef!** This reef is the largest coral reef in the world, stretching for more than 1429 miles or around 2300 kms. It is labelled as World Heritage Area. The Great Barrier Reef is the only living thing on earth visible from space.

WORD SCRAMBLE

R V E S L I   S L E L H

_ _ _ _ _ _   _ _ _ _ _

D W A N

_ _ _ _

L H E S I D

_ _ _ _ _ _

P C A E L A

_ _ _ _ _ _

HELP FAIRY FIND THE SHELL

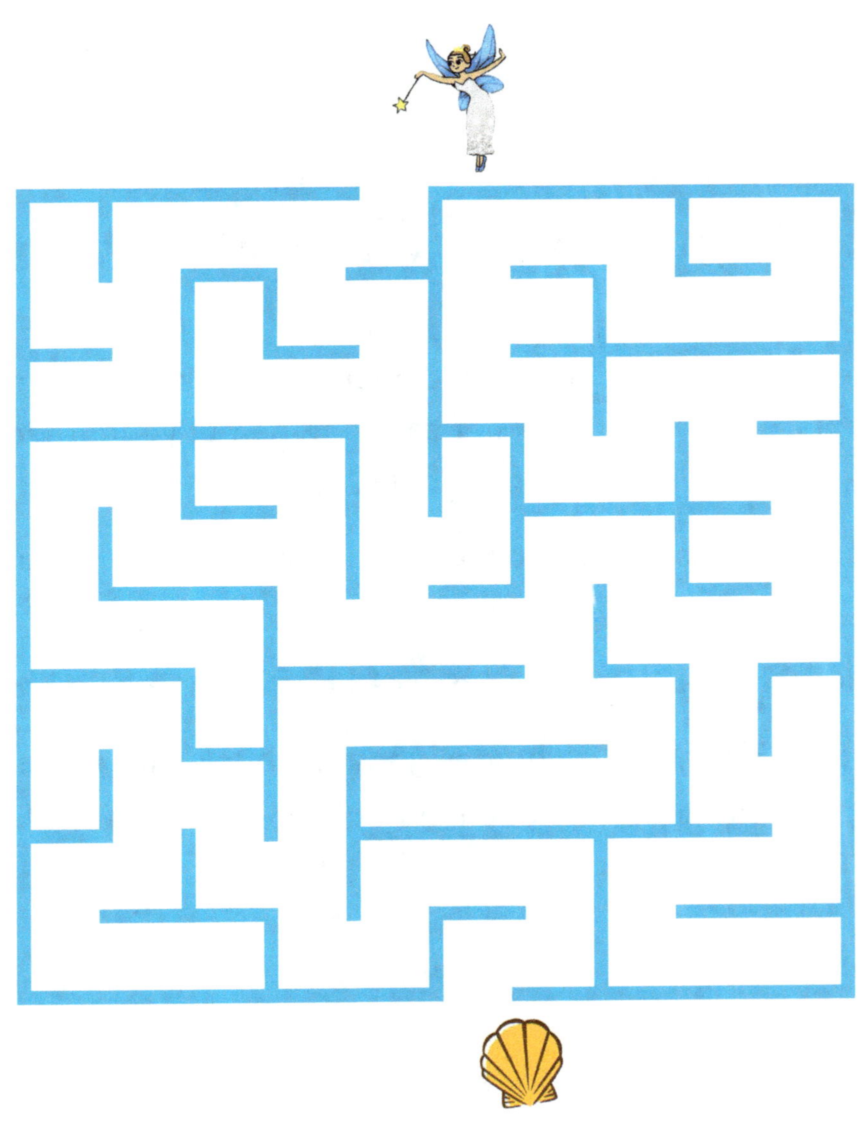

My special thanks to:

Mumma, thanks for helping and supporting me throughout the journey of book writing. The stories are mine but you turned them into books.

Papa, all this couldn't have been possible without you.

My editor, Li Ping, who edited my books with her usual fine eye to details. Her expertise and advice have been invaluable.

My illustrator, Ritwick Roy, who designed my book with patience and panache and rendered beautiful book cover and illustrations.